A NOTE TO PARENTS

Disney's First Readers Level 2 books were created for beginning readers who are gaining confidence in their early reading skills.

Compared to Level 1 books, **Level 2** books have slightly smaller type and contain more words to a page. Although sentence structure is still simple, the stories are slightly longer and more complex.

Just as children need training wheels when learning to ride a bicycle, they need the support of a good model when learning to read. Every time your child sees that you enjoy reading, whether alone or with him or her, you provide the encouragement needed to build reading confidence. Here are some helpful hints to use with the **Disney's First Readers Level 2** books:

★ Play or act out each character's words. Change your voice to indicate which character is speaking. As your child becomes comfortable with the printed text, he or she can take a favorite character's part and read those passages.

★ Have your child try reading the story. If your child asks about a word, do not interrupt the flow of reading to make him or her sound it out. Pronounce the word for your child. If, however, he or she begins to sound it out, be gently encouraging—your child is developing phonetic skills!

★ Read aloud. It's still important at this level to read to your child. With your child watching, move a finger smoothly along the text. Do not stop at each word. Change the tone of your voice to indicate punctuation marks, such as questions and exclamations. Your child will begin to notice how words and punctuation marks make sense and can make reading fun.

★ Let your child ask you questions about the story. This will help to develop your child's critical thinking skills. Use the After-Reading Fun activities provided at the end of each book as a fun exercise to further enhance your child's reading skills.

★ Praise all reading efforts warmly and often!

Remember that early-reading experiences that you share with your child can help him or her to become a confident and successful reader later on!

— Patricia Koppman
Past President
International Reading Association

Layouts by Judie Clarke
Pencils by Denise Shimabukuro and Scott Tilley
Paintings by Atelier Philippe Harchy

First published by Disney Press, New York, New York.
This edition published by Scholastic Inc.,
90 Old Sherman Turnpike, Danbury, Connecticut 06816
by arrangement with Disney Licensed Publishing.

SCHOLASTIC and associated logos are trademarks of Scholastic Inc.

ISBN 0-7172-8884-6

Printed in the U.S.A.

Mulan Saves the Day

Adapted by Nancy E. Krulik
Illustrated by Atelier Philippe Harchy

Disney's First Readers — Level 2
A Story from Disney's *Mulan*

SCHOLASTIC INC.

New York   Toronto   London   Auckland   Sydney
Mexico City   New Delhi   Hong Kong   Buenos Aires

There is a war in China.
Mulan's father can't fight. So
Mulan pretends to be a man,
to go in her father's place.

Mulan rides to the army camp.
Mushu the dragon goes with her.

Mulan meets Captain Shang.
It is his job to train the
new soldiers.

Mulan tries hard.
But she makes many mistakes.
Big mistakes!

The soldiers must climb a tall pole.
All the soldiers fail many times.
Finally, Mulan makes it to the top!

The enemy attacks!
Can Mulan and her
friends stop the Huns?

Clever Mulan aims the
cannon at the mountain.
Snow covers the Huns.
Hooray!

But Captain Shang is in trouble.
Mulan must pull him to safety.

Mulan is the bravest one of all.
But the men find out that she
is a woman.

They leave her alone on the
mountain.

And Mulan sees that the Huns
still live.

She must warn
the Chinese army!
    Once in the city,
Mulan uses her brain
to save the Emperor.